Trysts

Tales to mess with your sanity.

For Linda, may your new legs come soon.

Contents

The Bus Stops
Rheumy Eyes
His Reward
I Know What You Are Going To Do After
Reading This
Inflation
Read It And Weep
The Missing inks..
Jonathan (an indulgence)

All is not necessarily what it purports to be.

Books by Kim Clover

Return to the Broadwaters
Anguilla's Retribution
The Calling of the Scales
Kron
The Strange World of Kim
A Council Estate Creation
Dark Essence

The Stranger World of Kim
Transient
White Waters
The Reeds Have Eyes
Trouble Waters
Bargepoles and Boathooks (with Linda Clover)
A Box of Stuff

Trysts

Part One

Dark green, I will be wearing a dark green top and a black skirt.

Sarah looked at the words on the screen of her lap top and for a fleeting moment found her finger hovering over the 'delete' key.

No, she told herself, *you've done this too many times, got this far and chickened out.*

I will be carrying a black faux leather handbag. *Does he need to know that bit?*

Don't want any mishaps like him talking to the wrong lady, lots of us wear dark green tops.

Sarah spoke the words to herself but Milo picked up on the sound of her voice and looked up expectantly from his place on the carpet.

'Not you, you silly cat'

I have long brown hair and…

This time Sarah's finger found the 'delete' key.. *I have already told him that on the first contact page.*

Place and time of first meeting… We suggest a public place frequented by a large number of customers and a reasonably early time of the day.

Sarah read the printed advice for the fifth time and felt the same shiver of trepidation at the man's suggestion.

'How about the Woodsman..for about 21.30 pm?'

The Woodsman was a small pub on the outskirts of the village and was 21.30 pm a 'reasonably early time of the day'.

Oh, for god's sake Sarah, get a grip, do you need to meet with this man called Michael or not?'

Saturday was still 3 days away, she had plenty of time to change her mind.

Sarah hit send.

*

Dark green top and black skirt. Ok for 21.30 The Woodsman Saturday.

Alex read the first few lines and a grin spread across his thin lips.

So it's 14.30 with Alison in the red dress at The Duke, 18.30 Chloe in black at the Hogs Head, with a well needed break until 21.30 for whatever her name was in the green.

Gonna be a busy Saturday night.

He didn't think for one minute she'd go for 21.30 but obviously he underestimated his own charm and way with words.

*

Michael Mathewson 43 years old, widowed 7 years, house owner and comfortable lifestyle. Company Director and part time avid charity fund raiser.

Enjoys long country walks and lots of fresh air, foreign travel and collecting antiques and curios.

Michael enjoys the theatre, the cinema, the simple life and eating out.

Michael is looking for a lady with similar interest to help while away the lonely hours. Sarah read the short introduction for the hundredth time, smiled at Milo stretched out on the carpet at her feet and closed the laptop down…she would look at it again later no doubt.

*

Sarah Robson 39 years old, widowed 5 years. Own house and car. Works for the NHS as a health worker visiting the elderly and infirm in their own houses.

Alex couldn't be bothered with the rest of the text; he needed another beer from the fridge. The noise from the High Street was louder

than usual and because of the hot humid air all his second floor flat windows were wide open. Besides, if his luck held out he'd be sitting next to the green top on Saturday night.
Unless of course if he got lucky with...Alex held the mouse scrolled down quickly took a sip of warm lager from the can and on a protracted belch uttered the names 'Alison or Chloe'.

*

Alison, surname withheld, 48 years old divorcee. Ex P.A. now manager of a well known Garden Centre.
Enjoys reading, gardening, travelling and meeting people. Not afraid to try new adventures and places.
Dog owner loves animals.
Non-smoker, teetotal for 6 years.
Looking for friendship and possibly more if I find the right person, male or female.
Alex reads parts of two sentences again, nonchalantly flicking a cigarette butt out of the open window, his curiosity piqued.
'Not afraid to try new adventures'..'male or female'.

It wasn't getting any cooler in the small room. Alex left the laptop open and went to the kitchen for a fresh lager.

*

Chloe Butler a young 47 year old divorced mother of two young children from a previous marriage. Has part custody of said children. Alex almost deleted Chloe's details but hey, beggars can't be choosers.
Lives life to the full, loves dancing, parties, dressing up and mad people.
Has slight limp after a bad road accident 2 years ago.
Looking for a fun relasunship with the right type of bloke.
Alex ignored the spelling mistake, again beggars can't be choosers, besides this one sounds a bit of fun.

Part Two

Alex looked at his watch for the fifth time in as many minutes, 14.05 and took a sip of his barely touched half of lager..

It was always the worst time waiting, wondering if the lady was going to appear, *was going to show up,* especially when the barman kept glancing over and raising an inquisitive eyebrow.

He took the copy of the printout out of his jacket pocket and reread the details.

Alison, surname withheld, 45 years old divorcee. Ex P.A. now manager of a well known Garden Centre.

Enjoys reading, gardening, travelling and meeting people. Not afraid to try new adventures and places.

Dog owner loves animals.

Non-smoker, teetotal for 6 years.

Should be a cheap afternoon.

Alex folded the printout and put it back in his pocket.

Then took his wallet out of his trouser pocket and smiled as he slid one of the black and gold business cards he always carried and read the shiny embossed lettering.

Michael Mathewson.
Company Director.
Elston's Electronic Systems U.K.

14.23.
Alex's smile widened, he'd be Michael Mathewson again in less than ten minutes if all went well.

*

A tall man with long grey came through the pub's narrow glass and wooden door, he hesitated, stood back and held it open for the lady to step into the pub in front of him. She wore a red dress and an unmistakable nervous smile as her eyes scanned the room's dim interior.
Then after a short hesitation they settled on Alex's.
Alex immediately stood.
She looked quite nice from where Alex was sitting.

He looked presentable from where Alison was standing.

He took a step towards the lady in red and bumping his knee on the shiny brass surface of the table uttered a loud 'Ouch' Alison smiled.

They all smiled when he did that, *it never failed to break the ice..*

And then Alex was instantly Michael Mathewson.

*

Michael gestured to the chair opposite his, waited for her to sit and then took his own.

'Alison, I assume,' he uttered, taking his eyes with hers and using his best smile.

Alison smiled back, a tentative tight smile that never reached her own eyes.

'What can I get you to drink?'

'An orange juice with ice please, thank you'

Michael stood and made his way to the bar.

He didn't see the tall man with the long grey hair look over and wink at Alison.

He wasn't meant to.

Part Three

'It's nice to meet you, may I call you Alison ?'

Alex was speaking as he took his seat, placing the orange juice down, the ice clinking in the glass, his smile wide and he hoped engaging'

'Yes of course, please do and you are Michael I assume'.

Alison answered, ignoring the two packets of crisps Alex had laid on the table between them.

An embarrassing silence ensued as the two of them looked at everything but each other and when one of them found the voice the other one did at exactly the same time.

'I see you..'

'So you are a..'

Alex was quick to raise his palms in an apologetic gesture, a slight chuckle escaping through his smile..

'Sorry, please, you go on…Alison'
The pause before he added her name,
uncomfortably long.
'So, eh, how are you?'
As soon as the words left her mouth Alison
closed her eyes and bit her bottom lip.
What a stupid thing to say ?
'I'm fine thank you, and you?'
'Yes I'm..'
'We need to start again I think'
Alex's grin spread across his face, he
glanced at his watch, 14.36, it was going to
be a long afternoon.
*He looked at his watch, Alison definitely
saw him look at his watch.*
*She sighed a deep sigh and fought to
restrain herself from looking over at the tall
man with the long hair sitting by the window.*
She would have to do a lot better.

*

'Well, what do you think Bev, sorry Alison ?'
The tall man with the long grey hair closed
the door and couldn't resist a chuckle.
'From what I saw he looks like a total loser'

'You get the drinks, I'll get out of this bloody horrible red dress, put something comfy on and tell you all about the so-called Michael Mathewson'

Part Four

Christ that was hard work and his pokey little 2nd floor flat was still hot and humid at nearly 6pm.
Alex went to the fridge for a can of lager but thought better of it, maybe a coffee would be a more sensible idea.
Busy evening in store.
Pascoe, what a fucking stupid name for dog and didn't the bloody woman go on about it.
Forty eight years old, fifty five at least Alison my dear old girl'
Alex considered the T.V. but he would more than likely fall asleep in front of it.
Much better to recall some of the conversation with… Alison, it brought a smile to his face.

*'So Mathew being a Company Director must
be an exciting job ?'*
*'Yes, Alison it can be, as you say, exciting,
but very demanding'*
Good time to add something important Alex
my boy....*demanding.*
'I hope you don't mind Alison but I need to
be away by five at the latest. I hate to be
rude but…
Of course Alison had said.
Being a Company Director of Elstons
Electrical Systems U.K. must keep you very
busy, I fully understand.

*

'Is your Garden Center local Alison, would I
have heard of it?'
'No I don't think so Mathew, its..its a bit out
in the sticks'

*

'I thought you were tee total Bev'
The tall man with the long grey hair handed
her a glass with three fingers of malt whisky
and a wide grin on his face.

'Bev smiled herself looking up at him and taking the proffered glass'

'Do you know what I said when the creep asked me what my dog was called?'

'Couldn't hear a word where I was sat'

'Pascoe'

'Pascoe, where did that come from?'

'Same place as Allison I suppose'.

The man with the long grey hair and Bev tapped the two glasses together and laughed.

*

The car park of the Hogs Head was only half full.

Alex leaned his bike against the wall out of sight behind a dirty white transit van.

A glance at his watch told him it was 18.15.

He'd find a seat by the window and wait, he didn't have to for long.

The limp was only slight but it was nonetheless evident and she was wearing black.

Alex checked his printout, yep.

*

'Chloe?'

'Mathew?'

The initial introduction was succinct and made standing up.

'Can I get you a drink..?'

'A gin and tonic please'

Alex had made up his mind it was going to be a single before he'd even reached the bar.

Chloe sat down looking with vague amusement at the two packets of crisps lying in front of her on the table.

*

'I was lucky with the bus, it was bang on time'

Alex smiled as he put the glass and the bottle on the brass topped table.

'Thats good'

He didn't know what else to say.

Chloe glanced surreptitiously around at the smattering of other customers before speaking.

'I've got two kids you know'

'I know'

The silence went on for too long.

The rabble of the other customers' voices suddenly a welcomed diversion to both Alex and Chloe.

Alex thought he'd better say something encouraging.

'So I see you are a divorcee'

'Yep'

'With two kids' Chloe added quickly.

Alex had a quick vision of the delete key on his laptop.

Maybe he should have tapped it after all.

The gin and tonic was disappearing too quickly.

*

'I understand you have quite a high-powered job Mathew?'

Chloe had been rehearsing that question on the bus.

For a split second Alex forgot he was Mathew.

A swift sip of his lager and Alex's composure was restored.

'Yes Chloe, it can be quite demanding at times'

'Company Director of Elstons Electronics UK'

Chloe had been rehearsing that on the bus as well.

'I should imagine looking after two children is quite demanding as well'

'Only part time' Chloe added.

'I only have them part time'

Chloe was quick to reiterate.

Alex finally managed to find the delete button.

Chloe's bus home was bang on time too.

Part Five

It was just beginning to get dark but the lights in the car park were enough to see people occasionally arriving and leaving The Woodsman.

Sarah took the slip of paper from her black faux leather hand bag and smiled as she looked down at her blue patterned top. She glanced at her favourite photograph of Milo in the clear pocket in her purse and her smile widened.

The clock over the bar told her it was 21.10.

She fleetingly thought about the irony of being stood up and at that point the door of the pub opened and in walked the man that must be Mathew.

Good, the large lady at the bar had begun to give her strange looks.

The man that must be Mathew was making his way slowly to the bar eyeing up the seated customers as he went.

His eyes fell briefly on Sarah's then they were gone.

Alex was looking for a lady in a dark green top and black skirt.

*

That was a bonus they did his favourite lager. Alex looked at his watch, ordered a pint and two packets of crisps.
He had at least fifteen minutes.
Alex found a table and sat down.

*

When the tall man with long grey hair entered the pub with two young ladies walking either side of him Alex barely noticed them.
When the lady with the blue patterned top stood up to greet them Alex watched with avid curiosity.
When all three of the newcomers turned towards Alex, his table and the two packets of crisps the tall man with the long hair spoke.
'You must be Mathew?'
'No' answered Alex
'I think you've made a mistake, my name's Alex'

Population Explosion

The push chair had been on an incline so when the young woman's hands were no longer holding on to it, it rolled away onto the grass verge under the weight of its tiny occupant and came to a gentle halt. The child had been asleep until the left arm of its mother landed with a wet thud somewhere close on the concrete of the pavement. A fine spray of blood coloured the little boy's blond hair a strawberry pink and a large flap of his mother's loose warm skin landed like a heavy sodden blanket over his tiny legs. Further thudding sounds came to the infant's ears but by now he had begun to cry, a cry that carried to the people watching, the people standing rooted to the spot unable to take their eyes from the terror unfolding before them.

I too had been watching transfixed from the balcony of my apartment. It had been the first one I had actually seen. I was not actually *'looking'* if you know what I mean but when somebody explodes in front of your very eyes you *see it*, no, you *feel* it.

For a good few days now the televised news had been full of it, the front pages of every newspaper taken up with an abundance of horrifying stories and gory photographs. People were exploding, at random, their bodies bursting from the inside out, spewing their innards into the air and sending fragmented limbs in all directions.

'Scientists believe the phenomenon is caused by an airborne virus, scaremongers say it is part of a new wave of chemical warfare delivered by terrorists, some say it is part of an attack from alien life forms, air condition

buildings, get into air conditioned buildings, it can't get to you there"

The shouts are coming from all around me. I am running. In amongst a crowd of hysterical stampeding people I am running. The ground below me is slippery with blood and the expelled guts of others.

I try not to look at the riderless motorbike that is crashing into the wall to my left, the woman with the shopping bags screaming as a rain of gore soaks her from head to foot. Another thud, another limb falls in front of me, I skirt around it almost losing my balance.

The air conditioned library is only metres from me, my chest heaves as I run, I feel a popping noise in my ears I run, I feel my face getting warm , I can see the sign for the library but someone's erupted torso hangs over the last four letters in a shredded and bloody shawl

..Lib.. I'm getting nearer, nearer, almost there, my face is getting warmer, my heart is thumping in my chest...I'm almost there, I'm almost…

Trust

I knelt at her side and placed my open hand gently on her shoulder.
"Daddy ...."? Her voice was a small and timid sound and as she turned to face me and her eyes found mine, I felt a sudden shiver of disquiet anticipation...of guilt.. After all she would be the innocent one in all this. Am I going to hurt her? Am I going to expose her to what she does not deserve exposure to?
Even as these thoughts occurred I remained at her side with my hand on her

shoulder but now with my head turned from hers and my eyes searching for its imminent approach.

There was time yet, time to take her up in my arms and carry her away to where it could not affect her, to where she would not see it, feel it, have knowledge of it... we could go now....now...it is still not too late and then before I had time to catch my breath and tear her from its coming it *was* too late.

Too late. Around us the earth seemed to tremble and shake. She turned again to face me and her elfin features were contorted in a look of confused fear.

"Daddy!" she said no more, or if she did I ceased my listening and chose to hear nothing. I had betrayed her trust and I watched with a deepening feeling of shame as she placed both hands tightly to her ears in a vain attempt to shut out the terrifying all consuming noise that surrounded us both in its intrusive anger.

The Visit

'I don't remember the playground being this small'
She looked up at me with a coy smile on her face.
'It was over 10 years ago and you yourself were a lot smaller, you know what they say about Christmas trees'
I smiled back.
'I suppose so'
She took my hand.
'Come on, I'm dying to see inside'

*

The aromas assailed me like a hot summer breeze as the big wooden and glass swing doors closed behind my back.

Polish, disinfectant, mashed potatoes and probably only in my imagination chalk dust and powdered paint.

The Headmasters Office.

The gold lettering on the single door across the foyer was not as shiny as I remembered but the worn carpet leading up to it still bore the pattern I studied whilst standing still and shaking with trepidation.

'Come'

A tug on my hand and I was rescued from my reverie.

'Come on lets have have look in old Headmasters office, I never got to see inside it'

And then she looked up at me again with another coy smile.

'I know you did'
I smiled back, slipped my jacket off my shoulders and put it over a small wooden chair.
It was too hot a night to go exploring wearing it.

*

I expected the door to creak and a large cloud of bats to fly out as in all the old black and white horror movies.
Neither happened.
The room was in semi darkness, although the thick velvet curtains that hung from the wooden pelmets were opened wide.
Standing stately in one corner was a tall grandiose grandfather clock and against the windowed wall an empty leather chair tucked neatly between the carved legs of a solid wood writing bureau.

The small hand in mine gestured by a fleeting squeeze then I looked down into its owner's face.

She wriggled her nose and in that instant we could smell the old Headmasters long exhaled and extinguished aromatic pipe smoke.

We backed out of the room closing the door behind us, there were many other memories about us to explore, to taste.

*

Assembly.

Piano music and discordant juvenile voices.

'Onward Christian soldiers, marching as to war..'

'All things bright and beautiful..'

'He who would valiant be 'gainst all disasters..'

But now only…

Silent echoes from the arched oak beams high above the huge rooms polished and well trodden floor.

At one end a temporary stage, constructed of rectangular hollow blocks and partially hidden under heavily stained red drapes, the other end two sets of doors that opened out into a large area for gathering before entering.

Blazered school children surreptitiously chewing toffee and mints holding in grubby sticky hands well worn hymn sheets and bibles.

Scuffed shoes and ponytails.

She was pointing.

I followed her gaze.

A broken window.

An easily recognised although faded red cricket ball lying motionless in sprinkled broken glass below it.

*

Although the bell was silent and no longer echoing through the empty corridors or the long vacated classrooms, it was announcing to a multitude of hungry rumbling tummies it was time for dinner.

She led me down wide yellow edged steps into a vast airy hall.

We stood beside the rows of brightly coloured plastic and chromed legged tables, each one surrounded by uncomfortable identical looking tiny seats.

Where chair legs once scraped gratingly on the flooring tiles, cutlery cluttered and warm food steam rose to the strip lighting at the ceiling.

No more.

*

The many steps I once ran up with ease now caused me to pause and catch my breath.

She looked down at me from two of them up and that familiar smile played on her lips once more.

And then we were there.

The room that took up a whole floor.

A thousand, thousand musty and age dried books standing ceremoniously from the ground to the ceiling on uniformed shelves.

History, Geography, Science, English Literature, silver plagues with black etched letters secured to each section denoting the reader's selection.

As we walked through the silence I could not be sure if we were looking at the books or them, us.

*

C.5.

My old classroom had shrunk the desks and chairs with it. The blackboard grey with chalk powder residue and the far window that always had the blind drawn down on it had the blind drawn down on it.

The intricate wooden model of Shakespeare's black and white house stood proudly on its plinth under a cover of dust in the shadows.

Pen nibs dipped in inkwells, paper pages flicked open and hands put up in the air for questions to be asked.

And then the sound that seemed an age of yawnings to be heard.

'That bell is for my benefit alone'.

The words that would always follow.

*

'The janitor will be waiting for us at the gates with the keys' two suspected intruders apparently'

P.C. Williams turned to the driver as he replaced the radio receiver back on its cradle on the dashboard.

P.C. Mc Pherson took a hand from the police car's steering wheel and ran the back of it across his brow.

'Kid's, mucking about at 03.30 in the morning, you'd think we'd have better things to do'

*

'Closed for school 'olidays'
The janitor shielded his eyes from the car's headlights as he handed over a set of heavy keys on a metal loop. of steel.
P.C Williams took them with a swift nod of his head.

'Won't be long'
The two officers left the janitor to his mumblings and made their way across an eerily silent and vacant playground towards the school's large entrance doors.

'Better stay together on this one Dave'

P.C. Williams was somehow relieved his fellow officer spoke the words before he did.

The black windows of the large building edifice loomed high above them as the two police officers followed their torch beams into the bowels of the school.

*

'P.C. Williams'

The voice came from behind him, it was the sarge'

'Yes, sarge'

P.C. Williams stopped on his way to the station's canteen and turned on his heels..

What had he done now ?

He couldn't help thinking as he faced the sergeant's never smiling features.

The sergeant looked at the sheet of paper he was holding in his hand then raised his eyes, to P.C. Williams.

'That report of intruders in that old school a couple of weeks back you and P.C. McPherson attended, remember ?'

P.C. Williams cupped his chin in his hands and made it look as if he was given the question serious thought.

'Yes' Sarge, he replied trying to think what the problem could be.

'Yes I do sarge' he reiterated. 'False alarm as far as I can remember, we found nothing untoward and we searched all over the…

P.C. Williams did not get to finish his words as the sergeant interrupted..

'Strange that, when the school reopened a teacher found a school jacket in the Headmasters office with a name tag written in blue ink on the inside of the collar..

Richard Patterson..

'Stranger still when we checked the records apparently Richard Patterson and his sister Wendy were both killed in a car accident eight years ago.

Two Fingers of Whisky

Doesn't sound long does it, one hour and forty five minutes but when you have to wait that long to finally meet the girl of your dreams it feels like it's going to be a lifetime.
Well, when I say the girl of your dreams I mean she could be the girl of your dreams, my dreams.
You see I haven't met her yet, only spoke to her online but I somehow get the feeling she will be the girl of my dreams.
When we finally meet up.
I'll top my glass up.

*

One hour and thirty two minutes.
She told me online she likes dogs.

I haven't got one but maybe we could borrow someone else's and take it for a walk.

I'll drink to that.

Good job I've got another bottle in the cupboard.

I know there's still one hour and twenty minutes to go but I'll be on the safe side, I'll get off my arse and turn the TV off. I won't be able to hear my phone if she calls to cancel like all the rest have done. Oops.

'Damn, that was a waste of good whisky, all over the bloody carpet..better get a refill.

Good job the glass was only half full.

*

Times going quicker now.

So's the whisky, I'll be meeting Pauline soon, only one hour and ten minutes.

Or was it Paula ?'

'Nah, Pauline I'm sure.

Two more fingers, that's what whisky
drinkers say isn't it?'
I'll just have two more fingers.
Plenty of time.

*

Wonder what she looks like.
Online she says she is blonde and
something about dogs.
Only fifty five minutes and I'll find out.
If she turns up.

*

Pete in dispatch says she sounds great.
Says, if I can't make it can I let him know.
Fat chance of that.
That calls for another drink I say.
One half of a football match to go, forty
five minutes.
That's without extra time of course.
That would make Pete in dispatch laugh.
Where do you get 'em from he'd say.
Anyway Pete in dispatch doesn't even
know where I'm meeting her.

I wonder if she likes whisky.
I do.

*

Twenty two minutes to go.
Better get my shoes ready, can't meet
what's her name in slippers can I ?
That really would make Pete in Dispatch
laugh, me turning in Mc Donalds in my
slippers.
Just got time for another little swig.

*

What's wrong with the T.V. ?
Don't matter, I'm going out soon.
Double cheeseburger and french fries, I
wonder what fingamebob will have.

*

Ten minutes.
Time to get my arse in gear.
KFC is a good five minutes down the
High Street and I don't want to miss her.

Shopping

He was standing by the onions, mushrooms and tomatoes, try as I might, I couldn't help but do a double take.

No question about it, he was staring straight at me. Not just a fleeting glance but to my chagrin a meaningful stare.

The sort of stare that us women find distinctly uncomfortable.

And I would have felt far more uncomfortable if I hadn't been in a busy supermarket.

I made my way up the aisle to the cheese, milk and butter, forcing myself not to look behind me.

Soon I could turn the corner into back bacon and sealed ham.

Instincts told me he was still behind me, still looking.

I walked a bit faster past the intersection down to paracetamol, vitamins and cough syrup.

I said hi to a neighbour, Alice but nothing else, I don't like her.

Was the man still looking, yes he was by the end of the aisle where all the batteries and plug in chargers were.

I passed the section where they display a smattering of children's clothing, socks, bras and knickers.

Another intersection crossed and I was pretending to look at ready meals one side of me and frozen chicken breasts and pork loins the other.

For a moment I thought I'd lost the man but then I saw him with his back to the baked beans, cereals, sugar and flour with eyes only for me.

Jars of jam, marmite and peanut butter seem to pass me in a confused blur merging into crisps, pringles and beef jerky.

He was still there, making the distance between us less and less to background electric sound of bleep, bleep, bleep.

The smell of freshly baked bread and the sight of crusty rolls assailed me as I made my way to the canned lager bottled wine and wired against shoplifters' rows of spirits.

Nearly there, the tills, the cashiers and safety.

It was then I noticed the dog food, we don't have a dog.

And the man's voice at my side.

'Excuse me miss but I think you've got my trolley.

What a Shot ?

The ball from Dave was inch perfect it literally landed at my feet. I brought it under control with a tap from my right boot without losing any of my stride.

The crowd was a blur as I made my way up the right wing.

A deft swerve to my left took me around an advancing defender and to avert a second one's tackle I put it through his legs.

I only had the goalkeeper to beat.

I steadied myself, raised my right foot and sent the ball soaring into the top left hand corner of the net just teasing the goalkeeper's outstretched hand on its way.

The roar was incredible..

I woke up with a start to see the bedroom curtains flapping and a large jagged hole in the window.

I got out of bed and looked at the garden below.

A football lay on the lawn surrounded by shards of shattered glass.

The Book

I wasn't looking for it, in fact I wasn't looking for anything in particular, just browsing.

The strange little shop had somehow beckoned me in from the rainsoaked street, a curio come junk shop..

Concetta's Antiques and Curios

Shadowed, damp and full of dubious objet d'art it nonetheless held a certain temptation I just could not resist.

I vaguely remember the elderly lady reaching out with gnarled fingers to pick up the article, take my proffered money and toothlessly grin at me.

I walked out of the premises no more than five minutes later with it in a plastic shopping bag.

Such a mundane beginning.

'Dark Essence' the book was called.

Its faded fabric cover was frayed at the edges and stained and when opened its pages released a smell of age dried time itself. A musty aroma that spoke of late night card games, cigarette smoke, sour wine, of stale perfume and whisky dregs puddled at the bottom of greasy glasses. It bade me, read it.

*

It was quite a large tome, its pages numbered to 289, some dog eared and slightly creased but all intact.
It was later that evening when I found myself lying back and propped up against the headboard under the light of the bedside lamp my wife beside me engrossed in her own book.
The silence seemed fitting as I started reading, naively unaware of the dark place 'Dark Essence' was about to lead me.
'Alexander frowned, it was not what he had expected or wished to see, the windows in darkness. He strode towards

the large dirty window, the paint of its frames cracked and peeling, the sign above and just below the shop's roof faded and discoloured'.

The thought struck me that I had entered a similar premises earlier that day and purchased the book I had now in my hands.

Coincidence.

It wasn't long before I found myself turning the fragile pages and sinking into the books, long ago written tale.

The voice came from behind the stained pitted counter, in the semi darkness stood a wizened elderly lady, humped back, white haired and grasping in one gnarled hand a gold-tipped wooden cane.

I could visualise the old lady with the gnarled fingers, taking my money, handing me the old tattered book, grinning at me as she did so.

That night I would take it to bed with me and read it.

'Help me, whoever you are please help me, it will not release me, the standing stone has hold of my mind, it is taking my mind'. Alexander took a couple of tentative steps towards the figure on the bed when another voice, not carried to his ears on the air but deep in his own mind assailed him.

I was drifting in and out of sleep, the words and unknown names on the pages now making no sense, no sense at all. My wife had turned her light off and murmured 'good night darling' and was soon asleep, another nonsensical page and I would do likewise.

That's when the ancient looking hand written letter dislodged itself from somewhere deep within the book and settled itself on my pillow

My new Friend
With many good wishes to you. I read with you many good thoughts and feel it must be I write to yourself. I read many books from your hand and many items from magazines you write inside. You tell of many tales and stories of the evil of many things. The luck charms, talismans and amulets and the dooms of them. I have of such a thing. You tell

you no of the histories of such things and how to battle these things. I have a curse of old thing and my terrors are many. My son, Arne have death because of curse of old thing, they try destroy but no. You write you can destroy and not have death. I beg of you my new friend you have do what you write I have have much gratitude to you. I beg you please bring me your help.

*

I was now suddenly wide awake, wow, what does all that mean ?

Who is this new friend, who wrote this letter and to whom was it intended ?

The author of the book in my hands, Dark Essence maybe?'

I turned to the cover and saw an illegible scrawl where the author's signature should have been.

No answers. I found myself reading on, a senseless jumble of words with no direction but I was powerless to put the damned book away.

A woman's voice, imploring, beseeching, a man's sobbing, the scrapping of wooden bed legs against the floor all emanating from a stairway leading to the building's upper floor. Invisible to Alexander the large oak door at the top of the stairs slowly opened with its groaning hinges protesting at every determined push from behind. Elise stepped across its threshold and silhouetted starkly by the room's own light stood motionless in waves of hideous sobs that pulsed at her back. Below in the semi dark still sitting at the table and paralysed

with fear Lotte finally felt the presence
now standing at her side, she took her
hands from her ears and dared to look up.

Another page turned and my eyes were immediately drawn to hand written words in the empty space between the end of one chapter and the beginning of another.

All will become clear dear sir, do not fail me, read on, read on within the company of the dark essence.

What is this? Why cannot I not just close this wretched book and go to sleep, sleep as my wife does beside me?

Another page, more abstract and meaningless words and random unknown names.

'Help me, whoever you are please help me,
it will not release me, the standing stone
has hold of my mind, it is taking my mind'.

Alexander took a couple of tentative steps towards the figure on the bed when another voice, not carried to his ears on the air but deep in his own mind assailed him.

I would lie back and try to calm myself, ignore the printed words but sleep would not come, my brain was in an incredulous turmoil and for reasons I could not fathom sleep would not come.

Dark Essence held me and refused to release its omnipotent will over what I was beginning to fear was my sanity. With my hands numb and unmoving I watched in fearful awe as the pages turned themselves, slowly, slowly, allowing me to absorb each and every nonsensical sentence.

'I believe that it is incredibly rare for any object to radiate any form of 'dark essence' to an unreceptive person or persons, having said that a person given the gift wanted or unwanted of such receptiveness could easily succumb to the 'dark essence' emitted'

This 'dark essence' had manifested itself with an actual physical strength, he had previous knowledge of it and with that came certain unaccountable sensations he had never experienced before, he would need to fight to overcome them...

'What is happening to me Dr. Alesandro, what in hell's name is happening to me, am I being visited upon by a 'dark essence' Dr. Alesandro, that is what you believe isn't it, that is why you answered my letter by being here, isn't that exactly it Dr.

Alesandro?' Can you help me Dr....I fear I am losing my mind, please tell me what it is that is doing this to me.'

And with the coming of the new day and the last remaining pages of the book a realisation seeped into my slowly awakening mind. As the light through the lace curtains won its battle over the darkness I became finally aware that the dark essence had no doubt visited me.

The dark essence was the book itself.

Today I would destroy it.

No birdsong, no sound, just imagined silhouettes in the clinging mist of long ago, mourners their shoulders slumped, their eyes down, black top hats of the men and the black net veils of the women lowered to cover alabaster and tear stained faces.

The rector at their head standing solemn, an opened book in his hand trailing a red ribbon from its pages, his mouth opening and closing in silent lament. And on the gravel path the carriage, its single horse frozen in time, a plume standing erect on its head, its silver bit glinting in the moonlight...

Lex Talionis

'Dan, Dan, get up and come down here, now'

His mothers voice came to him from downstairs and it carried with it an unmistakable sound of urgency.

Dan looked at the clock on his bedside table 08.15 and was just about ready to protest *that it was a bloody Saturday and..*when the voice came again and if anything sounded more urgent, more insistent.

'Dan, get down here now the police are here'

'The police, Dan's mind went straight to the night of the fireworks he and Mickey had let off outside the school... *shit.*

Pushing the blankets off his legs Dan was out of bed and rummaging around on the bedroom floor for his crumbled jeans.

'Now', Dan, I said now'

This was serious.

*

'Yes I know Bella Baily'

The policeman looked huge in the small lounge, the silver buttons on his tunic were bright and Dan made a point of looking at them and nowhere else, especially at his mother standing hands on hips in the kitchen doorway.

'But we call her Bossy Bella'

Dan was not quite sure why he added that.

*

'Tell me, son, when was the last time you saw...?'

The policeman paused, consulted a notebook in one of his massive hands and was speaking again.

'When was the last time you saw Miss Bella Bailey?'

'What is this all about?'

It was Dan's mother and as she spoke she took a step towards her son and the policeman.

'Just let him answer my question, again the policeman consulted his notebook..Mrs Williams'.

The policeman had lowered his notebook and fixed his eyes on Dan's.

'Well?'

Dan glanced at his mother.

So it was nothing to do with fireworks and all to do with Bossy Bella.

Dan's voice was a mere whisper.

'Yesterday, me and Mickey Davies saw her yesterday

'Yesterday' reiterated the policeman before adding..

'Where and when, I want the whole truth now'

And the truth was what the policeman got in Dan's faltering voice.

Bossy Bella is exactly that, bossy, everybody at school will tell you that, so me and Micky thought we'd teach her a lesson, take her down a peg or two, she was always bullying the younger girls.

Mickey and I had been messing about near the old haunted house in the woods when we found a big rusty key in the long grass. Micky said he wondered if the key was a key to the old haunted house.

I remember thinking he may be right, we should try it.

Nobody we know has ever set foot in that old house even during the day. It's well off the beaten track and not many adults even know it's there.

We tried the key in the haunted house's door and it opened.

I'm not lying when I say neither of us dared to walk more than a few steps into the building and from somewhere in the shadows we were both sure we heard loud blood curdling screams.

That was it. We walked swiftly away down the narrow track and out into the park.

That's when we saw Bossy Bella, she was all on her own sitting on a park bench, *Bossy Bella was always on her own..*

That's when we had the idea how to teach her a lesson *'Some of her own medicine'*

Micky said, nudging me and laughing..'I've got a great idea' he said, *'hurry up follow me before she goes'*

We broke into a run towards her, exaggerating our breathing for dramatic effect.

As we neared Bossy Bella reacted to our approach by quickly getting to her feet, she had little time for boys, Bella had little time for anyone.

'Wait, wait Bella' Micky was shouting between large gulps of air, 'Wait'

I watched as Bossy Bella paused and eyed us suspiciously..

'What could two crazy schoolboys want with me?'

The expression was written all over her face.

And then we were standing, panting before her and Micky was talking.

He told her that there was an injured puppy in the old haunted house and would she help us find it

It was a great idea, we'd get her to enter the old house with us and quickly run out..lock her in and leave her there all on her own for a while.

See how Bossy Bella is then.

'Yes, of course' she said 'poor thing, as long as you come with me, noway I'm going in that house on my own, not even in broad daylight'

Part Two

The police car was parked outside his house and as he lay his bike against the side wall Micky was hoping he'd see them dragging the Richardson's out of the house next to his again.

The paper round seemed to take ages today and his belly was aching for his breakfast. No school today thank God.

He heard voices as he walked along the narrow garden path towards the front door, male voices, stern voices, the hairs on the back of his neck were bristling. He had no idea why.

No sooner had he opened the door to his house than his fathers voice echoed loudly from behind the door to the lounge.

'Michael, is that you get yourself in here right this minute, someone here wants a word or two'.

The policeman was standing just inside the room, in comparison his father looked tiny sitting on the sofa.

'Michael this..'

Micky's father got no further; the policeman's voice boomed out from somewhere in his bushy beard.

'Just a few questions to help us with our enquiries young lad'

Micky's mind raced and a furtive glance at the stern features on his dads face did nothing to allay his growing trepidation.

What the hell has happened?

'I'll get straight to the point my lad' the policeman's eyes were piercing and the look on the bearded man's face was far too serious looking for Micky's liking.

'A young lady by the name of Bella Bailey has not been seen since yesterday afternoon and inquiries have led us to believe that the last persons to see her were yourself and a young gentleman by the name of Dan Williams..I therefore..

Micky Davies had never sworn in front of his father; it would not have been a good idea to do so.

'Fuck' he said.

*

The police found the key where the two boys said they had left it, under a slab of concrete at the side of the narrow track leading to the house.

Their stories were corroborated. They were to leave the screaming Bella Bailey in the house alone for only a few minutes and then one of them would return and let the terrified girl out. Which one they couldn't quite remember but they each assumed the other would.

Alan Mathews was in the park with his model airplane.

It was great fun watching him fly it.

*

The police found the key exactly where the boys had said they had left it.

But a thorough search of the building revealed there was no sign of Bella Davies anywhere..

She was never seen again.

Old Buddy

'Well blow me down, it is you isn't it?'

The man standing before me offering his hand out for me to shake was huge.

'Dave Metcalf as I live and breathe I haven't set eyes on you for what, twenty, twenty five years'

We shook hands vigorously.

'Someone told me you emigrated to Canada, or was it Australia, somewhere a long way away anyway'

'Now who told me that ?' 'Could have been your old mucker, Pete Bannister, or thinking about it probably that lass you were keen on, whatever her name was I can't remember, red hair, I can remember she had red hair, long and straggly'

'Did you hear about our old headmaster Parry?' Dirty bastard, he kept all that business quiet didn't he?'

'Well I can't be chatting to you all day Dave, got a lot do today, meeting up with Keith and..whatsisname'.

'Take care, old buddy see you around'

And then the huge man I've never seen before in my life was gone.

Final Train to Selby

25th August 1927.

Would I have boarded that train in Leeds had I known what that simple journey would entail ?

In retrospect I could have easily waited for a later train; they were quite frequent after all.

But in retrospect the very idea of that is ludicrous, academic, nonsensible.

I had no prior comprehension of what was about to befall me on that train..How could ? I am not clairvoyant.

I'm sure she was though.

Marianna.

*

With over a little more than ten minutes before departure from Leeds City Station I boarded the train and found a seat by the window and watched as more and more passengers boarded.

Within five minutes the train was quite full and I realised I would not be sitting alone for long.

And then with little decorum or regard to our situation she sat down next to me.

Marianna.

Of course I didn't know what the woman's name was at that precise moment, she was just a female travelling that happened to be on the same train as myself.

At first I could not identify the strong smell that emanated from her person and then all of a sudden I could..incense.. almost overpowering.

*

'I'm travelling to meet with my father Sir'

The train's wheels had not yet started to move and much to my surprise I realised the complete stranger sitting next to me had turned to face me and was actually addressing me without any prior communication or introduction.

'Sir, pray tell, are you visiting with anyone?'

Not to encourage any sort of further dialect between us I just replied in the negative, it did not dissuade her.

'My name's Marianna Sir'

She was holding out a tiny hand veiled in a black lace fragile looking mitten.

Not wanting to appear rude I took it gently, gave it the smallest shaking movement and swiftly released it.

From somewhere out on the platform a whistle sounded and the train's sudden initial jerking movement was enough to distract us and I was thankful that I had escaped the moment when revealing my own name seemed only polite.

I turned my head away as if all of a sudden I had found something interesting to look at through the train's windows and saw nothing but clouds of dense white smoke billowing past.

She was now speaking to my back.

'I believe my father is expecting me of course'

I was happy that what she had said required no answer from myself.

But my relief would prove to be short-lived.

'Where Sir are you travelling to, may I ask ?'

The train was picking up speed and my feeling was that it was not yet going fast enough.

'Selby' I replied and immediately felt misgivings for rudely answering the woman's reasonably valid inquiry with my back turned to her.

It was remiss of me and I regretted my behaviour but I could not bring myself to feel comfortable with the forthright liberties the woman was taking.

It was one thing to sit together totally unacquainted but..

'What a coincidence Sir, Selby happens to be my final destination also'

I did or said no more than give the woman the briefest of nods and a shadow of a smile.

The train began to lose speed and the tempo of its wheels on the rails made subtle changes, we were arriving into Cross Gates.

At a complete standstill and my hope that a number of passengers would alight the train and the woman would avail herself of another seat did not come to pass. In fact to my utter chagrin the complete opposite occurred and the air inside the carriage became all the more stifling for it.

*

The whistle sounded and I caught a glimpse of the uniformed guard waving his flag above his head seconds before he was engulfed in a thick cloud of smoke.

Just as I dared to believe that the woman who had the gall to invade my private space would at least be silent for the remainder of the journey her voice assailed my ears yet again.

'Can I assume, Sir, that Selby is your town of residence or are you like myself only visiting?'

I could feel her eyes searching my face, her breath held in wait for my verbal response. I regard myself as a charitable being and therefore I find it more than difficult to be dismissive of others.

I was committed to answering the woman's impertinent query.

'Madam, I am as yourself calling on relatives, I do not reside in the town of Selby'

That, that should be the cessation of a one sided conversation I could only hope.

But my hope was soon dashed.

'Such a quaint market town, I do enjoy my occasional visits and you Sir do you visit often?'

'No madam'

Was my succinct reply.

And as the train began to lose speed once again as we approached Garforth and I was grateful to be treated to a few moments of silence.

*

The whistle denoting our departure from Garforth was barely audible as the woman amplified her voice to be over it.

'I fear Sir that these vehicles of transport are not as clean as maybe they should be'

For reasons totally beyond me the woman had laid a lace covered finger across the rough material of her seat and was now staring intently at the thin layer of dust thereon.

I made no answer grateful that the distance between Garthforth and East Garforth was only a matter of minutes and the train had already begun to slow.

*

He made his entrance into the carriage through the narrow door with his head held high, his cap squarely on his head and his gait almost regimental.

'Tickets please'

I felt movement at my side as the woman searched her black lace purse for her ticket.

While the woman was concentrating on the matter at hand she was not conversing or attempting to converse with myself for which I was immensely grateful.

The train came to a jolting halt and the outside world was momentarily obscured by the inevitable white and grey smoke.

East Garforth.

*

And in the relative silence the woman's increasingly annoying voice rang out once more.

'May I be so bold as to ask you the time Sir, in my haste to breakfast and prepare myself for today's journey I appear to have forgotten my watch?'

Without pause and I'm afraid more than obviously noticeable irritance I retrieved my pocket watch from its place in my waistcoat pocket and glanced at its gold hands.

'A quarter of two madam'

An echo of a shrill whistle and we were once again moving.

*

Silence, from the seat beside me came the blissful sound of silence and just as I was starting to enjoy its welcomed company the voice that I had somehow become so unavoidably accustomed to again rang out.

'It's promising to be a fair day weatherwise Sir, I can see the sun as it appears between the light smattering of clouds'

To my utter disdain and disgust the woman was leaning across my person actually making contact shoulder to shoulder so as to look out of the train window, *my window.*

This was too much, too much for me to allow or be subjected to and I could not withhold my sudden angst or utter my enforced rebuke.

'Madam'

We had arrived at Micklefield.

*

He had once again made entrance to our carriage through the narrow door, his demeanour severe, his countenance one of consternation.

'Ladies and gentleman I am profusely apologetic to announce a slight delay in our onward journey from Micklefield, I am reliably informed that the delay will be only of a few minutes and we will be underway as soon as possible'

Audible moans of discontent and displeasure filled the carriage, none louder or more heartfelt than mine own.

*

Not that the woman needed any excuse to once again address me directly she nonetheless grasped at this opportunity.

'Oh what a carry on, this is not at all convenient and I'm sure dear Sir you are of the same opinion'

'Dear Sir, dear Sir' !!

This woman is surely taking outright liberties to the extreme, I could do no more than totally ignore her blatant impudence.

'I will surely demand a rebate on the cost of my travel which I hasten to add was all things considered unduly extortionate'.

There was no response required for her statement so I gratefully kept my silence until..

'What say you Sir?'

And then as if it came to my rescue the white and grey smoke once again appeared at the train window and the juddery sensation of movement filled my being.

Selby could not be far and would bring me nothing short of blessed euphoria.

'I believe we are near to our destination Sir'

The woman had begun to fidget in her seat, no doubt in preparation of our disembarking'

The white wooden sign with large black letters neatly painted on it became visible through the dirty windows and the train jerked to a complete standstill.

SELBY.

25th August 2025.

And my extreme relief was palatable as I stood back to allow the woman access to the carriage's centre aisle.

I was now once again carrying the mantle of a gentleman.

*

The platform was oddly devoid of any passengers and my attention was drawn to a single wisp of white grey smoke drifting over the empty rails that was all that was left of the train.

It had vanished from view.

And then in my peripheral I caught sight of a lone bent and ancient figure stooping in the shadows staring in my direction.

Our direction.

He began to wave a single hand in the air.

'Marianna' the man shouted, his voice distant, an ethereal sound.

Unbeknownst to me the woman was standing at my side.

'My father Sir' she said.

'My long since departed father'

'He can now only see the dead'

'Sir'

Two Desperate Men

The gun was hidden in the old grandmother clock standing at the end of the landing. He knew it was there but he wasn't sure if he could reach it without the two men seeing him.

They were both professional killers and they were out for his blood of that he had no doubt.

The house was silent apart from the sound of the ever on radio in one of the downstairs rooms..the house was big with bay windows and bare wood flooring.

It was no good he had to make a move or it could be too late, these men were desperate.

With his back to the wall he made his way step by step sideways up the narrow dark stairwell.

The sound of the radio getting quieter and more remote with every riser he ascended.

A shadow across the long landing, he stood completely still, his heart thumping in his chest.

And then the sound of muffled talking, followed by footsteps.

They were searching for him.

He needed to act fast.

*

He was on the landing, door ways to either side disappearing into the shadows the further down the corridor they went.

His senses told him the men had split up and were visiting each room separately.

He would have to act quickly, his life was in the balance.

The men were good at what they did. Hired assassins, professional murderers.

It was now or never, he would make a dash for it, with any luck he could get past any open door before either one the men had the chance to react.

And then he was running, running for his life towards the old grandmother clock and his hidden gun.

*

Ignoring the sounds of footfalls and threatening shouts from different directions he made a final darting leap towards the old grandmother clock, almost knocking it back against the bay window behind it.

He grabbed at the little wooden door in the side of it, yanked it open and closed his fist around the cold steel of his .38 loaded magnum.

A thudding footstep on wooden floorboards directly behind him, in an instant he was on his knees, a flash, a deafening roar and the man flew backwards a bloody hole in the middle of his forehead, he was dead before he hit the floor.

A shout, a slamming door, the blurred shadow of an fist holding a gun appearing from a doorway, a shot and the sound of a bullet passing inches from his cheek.

He heard the bullet embedded itself in the plaster behind his back.

With lightning reflexes he threw himself sideways to the floor, rolled his body over twice, took aim and put two bullets into the man's stomach.

He smiled as he stood but the smile was quick to disappear when the female voice from downstairs reached his ears.

'For heaven's sake Michael what's all that noise up there? Come down and have your porridge before it gets cold'.

The Bus Stops

She never liked him, he was too cocky, too know it all, She would need to take him down a peg or two.

And in front of others.

'Let me set you an arithmetic and confidence test Alan, you can use a calculator if you like'

'I won't need a calculator miss, calculators are for idiots'.

Cocky, know it all.

Ok, listen carefully. The other 8 year olds gathered around.

'A bus driver leaves the bus depot in his empty bus to travel to the first bus stop. Four people get on.

At the next bus stop five people get on.

He drives into the market area bus stop where three people get on and two get off.

Near the centre of town there is a large crowd sitting on the bench of a covered bus stop, eight people get on four get off, a passenger helps another young lady with two children in a pushchair get on the bus.

This is easy, says Alan.

Over the river bridge the bus stops and three people get on and no one gets off.

The bus stops at the New Inn pub and a crowd of four lads get on helping an elderly lady as they do, three people get off.

Soon they will be at the bus's final destination.

'Thats a pity says Alan, its just becoming easier'

Outside the park and on a roundabout the bus driver slows for a man standing at a temporary bus stop but the man waves the bus on.

Down the steep winding hill at the bus stop with the vandalised pole the bus driver stops, seven people get on and four get off.

Just off the short stretch of dual carriage way and the bus driver has stopped at a bus stop and has turned off his engine, he is running a little ahead of schedule.

While the bus is stationary three people board it.

'How are you doing Alan, are you ready to answer my question?'

'Of course I am miss'

'Ok, how many bus stops did the bus stop at?'

Rheumy Eyes

'Oh fucking marvelous, rain, that's all we need'

The words were barely out of his mouth before he felt old Bill's rheumy eyes on him, he lowered his own and didn't have to wait too long for the deserved admonishment he knew was coming.

'Respect, Stan, how many times do I have to tell you a little respect'

Stan glanced over at Ray and chanced a quick grin.

Ray in turn looked at Bill, saw he was looking up at the darkening skies and then winked at Stan.

And a gusty wind joined the rain to make the three men even more miserable than before.

*

'A quick one or two in the George after this one Stan?'

'Do bears sh..'

'Ray, watch your tongue' Bill's voice rang out.

And Ray was instantly silenced.

All three men were silent in the silence before Bill spoke again.

'You know I might even join you fella's tonight I could do with a warm up by the log fire in the George and a swift dram'

Another knowing grin was exchanged between Ray and Stan, neither man pointing out that Bill joining them in the George was by no means a rare occurrence.

And then Bill was speaking over the strengthening wind.

'Lets get this one finished sharpish, its getting darker by the minute and that rain is soaking through my anorak'

'Not arguing with that boss' responded Ray.

*

'No way was that a penalty last night'

Stan raised a wet sleeved arm and wiped the rain from his face as he spoke.

'Aston Villa were bloody lucky'

Ray glanced quickly at Bill, either that he hadn't heard him or for once the old man had decided to ignore the swearing.

*

'Do you reckon Judy will be behind the bar tonight?'

Ray's question was directed at Stan but both men chuckled when Bill was first to respond.

'Hope so' he said before adding...

'Come on lads, should have had this one nearly finished by now'

'So, your Wendy's up the duff again is she?'

Ray scratched a dirty finger across his shiny wet bald patch before replying to Stan.

'Three months she say's'

Bill's sigh was long and heavy.

'That's four now aint it ?'

Bill's next sigh was longer and heavier.

*

'They left the big cardboard box right outside their flat door, the bloody Coopers, leaning against the wall, Panasonic Widescreen splattered all over it in big black letters'

Ray had to raise his voice over the growing sound of the wind, he looked through the rain at Stan and then at Bill hoping for one of the men to react the way he was hoping they would, smiling to himself when Stan did.

'Showing off that's all mate, *look what we've got its got a 43" screen'*

Ray was silent for too long before muttering under his breath 'Said on the box 50" Screen'

Bill suppressed a giggle and once again ignored swearing, he realised he was getting more tolerant in his old age.

*

'No way that was a penalty last night'

Said Ray.

And then the long awaited and welcoming sound of three spades thudding against compacted earth and three men turned towards the narrow path that led out of the church towards George.

'Ow many we got tomorrow?'

Asked Ray.

'Four' replied an old man with rheumy eyes'

His Reward

The cloying stench was thick and abundant and strongly assailed his nostrils so he was more than convinced he was nearing its source.

Broken glass, splintered wood and sharp stones littered the uneven ground.

Here and there, there were ponds of shallow muddied water surrounded by mounds of thick oozing mud.

The rain that had earlier been a deluge was now no more than a light drizzle.

The unwanted, unnecessary light had long since faded to a twilight and the shadows were all the time thickening.

His innate senses told him he was not being pursued, he was safe out in the open for the time being.

Grasses and weeds grew in clumps and between outcrops of low bushes making progress slower than he would have liked but the aching in his empty stomach forced him to continue on with growing determination.

Over exposed tree roots and larger mounds of dried earth he was forced to jump, down troughs and up peaks he was careful not to lose his footing.

A sudden rustling sound caused him to pause his movements, hold his breath and crouch down.

It was no more than a gust of wind from high above.

He willed himself forward, urged on by the strong and enticing odours now so much stronger, so much nearer.

And then in a glimmering pool of rare moonlight the familiar sights of congealing blood and decomposing flesh met his tiny bulging eyes.

A furtive glance from side to side and satisfied he was completely alone, for now, he scurried into the fragile light towards his reward.

He fed satisfyingly on the soft carcass, with his long tensile tail wrapped around his body for comfort, his whiskered snout digging deeper and deeper into exposed muscle and sinew his long pointed incisors snapping easily the brittle bones.

I know what you are going to do after reading this.

Someone told me the bus was due in about twenty minutes.

That's right and usually it's on time, you new around here?

Yes we moved in around two weeks ago, we like it.

We've been here twenty years, don't think we will ever move.

What area do you live in ? Is it far from here?

The Southcote Estate, only a couple of miles down London road.

Yes, I've got an old friend who lives there, Alison Bradshaw.

Blonde woman, tall, has about six children, married to a policeman.

A small world isn't it ? I went to school with her

Is that the bus just coming over the hill over there?

No, that one goes to the other side of the town.

I hope it doesn't rain, I've left my umbrella at home.

It hasn't been forecast but I agree it looks really ominous.

We were thinking of going to the old abbey tomorrow sometime.

It's well worth a visit and you don't have to pay.

I'll ask the kids and see if they want to go.

I'm sure they'll really love it lots to see and do.

Have you been to the museum yet? That's worth a visit.

We thought we'd go there on Wednesday, if they were open.

Yes, they are open all week apart from Sunday of course.

Oh good I think that must be the bus at last.

Do you ever think of really weird facts? I sometimes do.

No I can't say I do, what makes you say that?

Do you realise that all our sentences have contained eleven words?

No, that's amazing, I wonder if anyone else noticed that fact.

Shouldn't think so but I bet they are all counting now.

Inflation

I don't know what's wrong with me lately, I feel so deflated.

There was a time when I looked down on the world and nothing could touch me.

I was full of life and felt invincible.

I could join in with games, bouncing from one adventure to another.

People of all ages would look up to me, people would reach up to me, all smiling as they did so.

Little children would marvel at me, point at me, smile at me.

I was the life and soul of the party.

I now feel so deflated.

Being a balloon isn't all it's blown up to be.

Read it and Weep

1837 the man said, it was published in 1837.

188 years old I replied without hesitation, which surprised me because mental maths was never my strong point.

I handed over the money he asked for which also surprised me, I don't normally buy books.

I'd only gone into the huge emporium to get out of the rain.

Or was it the book?

Reading me instead of me reading it.

*

'Shakespere, I had no idea you were into Shakespere'

Sally had taken the huge well worn tome from my hands and was weighing it on her own.

"It looks very old," she said, opening it out and inhaling the aroma of dusty time wafting from its yellowed and fragile pages.

'188 old years' I replied.

'What are you to do with it, may I inquire ?'

'It called to me Sally, from its high shelf in the emporium betwixt the books of Christopher Marlowe, Francis Beaumont, Thomas Kyd, Edmund Spenser, Thomas Middleton..'

'I had no choice but to buy it Sally, don't you ever see anything that you feel you should have, must have, would have ?'

Sally was staring at me open mouthed. She closed the book and as if it had suddenly burnt the skin of her hands she handed it back.

I swiftly took it from her, opened it at a random page and started to read aloud a snippet of its faded script.

'The jewel that we find, we stoop and take it. Because we see it but what we do not see we tread upon and never think of it. You may not extenuate this offence for I have had such faults but rather tell me...'

'Doesn't make any real sense to me'

Sally had picked up the empty coffee cups and was making her way to the kitchen with them.

I spoke to her back as she walked away.

'Well I intendeth to broaden mine own mind and readeth this front to backeth'

I heard Sally laugh as she rinsed the cups.

You do that love she said at least it will keep your mind off the horses.

*

For the rest of that day and most of the next I began to read and study the book. I would say looking back it became an obsession, the more I read the more I wanted to read.

'Don't forget darling, we're meant to be popping over to Simon and Diane's tomorrow night'

Sarah was putting on her coat to go shopping, I was sitting in the lounge with the book open on my lap.

'W'rry not mine own loveth i hast not f'rgotten i shall beest eft'

'Oh for God sake David why don't you put that silly book away and do some useful'

I smiled as I heard the door close, I closed the book.

Time for a coffee before the racing on the T.V…

I loved Saturdays.

*

Simon opened the door to us, Sarah was behind him in the hall with a wide greeting smile on her lips.

Mum, Dad come on in I'll get you both a drink, white wine for you mum, red for you dad?'

Bless her she always said that.

Simon took our coats.

The evening went too quickly.

'Well that was a lovely evening darling, 'said Sally as we climbed out of the taxi.

'T c'rtainly wast and most wondrous to heareth about Sarah being childling once more'

'Oh for fucks sake David don't start that again'

The taxi driver gave us both a funny look as I handed over a twenty.

*

We didn't speak much that evening, I couldn't put my finger on why but Sally seemed to be distant as well as a little short tempered.

I ignored her as best I could, keeping my nose buried in my old book. I was beginning to understand more and more of it.

And then Sally was talking.

'I thought I'd go down to Southampton, Tuesday, take mum out shopping, maybe stay a day or two'

'Yond wouldst beest valorous f'r thee i bethink thee shall enjoyeth being with thy moth'r'fr a while. I'll taketh thou to the station if't be true thee liketh'.'

And now Sally was shouting.

'Right that's it David, I have had enough of your stupidity, I'm going to bed'

'Wherefore art thee so fell mine own loveth, what hast i done to vex thee so much?'

Sally didn't reply; she just slammed the door and made her way up to bed.

I thought it wise to leave her to simmer down before I joined her, I was beginning to worry about her state of mind, maybe she should see Dr. Maxwell.

I would sit and read more of my fascinating old book.

*

I had looked all over the house for it, behind the sofa, on top of the fridge, I even looked in the loo in case I had taken it in there when I went..but it was nowhere to be seen.

'Sally hast thee seen mine own fusty booketh anywh're I hast nay idea wh're it couldst beest i wonder..?'

Sally answered my question before I'd finished asking it.

'No' she said.

I found my book later that evening when I went to put the rubbish out, luckily it wasn't too badly soiled.

*

Well yond all i rememb'r of the beginning of the endeth three months ago..Sarah hath walked out nev'r to cometh backeth i shall leaveth thee with thy accurs'd booketh the lady spake off.

The Missing inks..

I have ooked a over the p ace, the ounge, the kitchen, the bedrooms, even the bathroom, I just cannot find them any here.

 hen Sa y came into my room to ask me hy I as making so much noise I as far too embarrassed to te her.

She gave me a funny ook, smi ed, eft a cup of coffee on my tab e and c osed the door quiet y behind her.

I'm sure they ere there this morning because I as riting a etter to my brother and had not encountered any prob ems.

I've orked out there are on y t o missing but it is sti proving to be intense y annoying not to mention irritating.

You might say it can't be too bad because the t o that are missing aren't used that much but that's not the point.

I've never had to go ithout them before and I'm not sure hat to do now.

I rang my friend Bob, he to d me it has never happened to him, he sympathised

ith my di emma but could offer no reso
ution.

I I have to go through the rest of my ife
with them both missing ?

i I have to make do with the ones I sti
have eft?

That's hen the thought struck me.

A terrib e thought. If I've a ready ost t o,
hat's to prevent me osing more ?.

hat if I ake up tomorrow and discover
more are missing?

No, I rea y can't d e on it.

Going through the rest of my ife ithout
the t e v e and t enty third etters of the a
phabet is too dire to contemp ate.

Oh e I guess hat i be i be !!

A Bargain

'Ok, twenty I'll let you have it for twenty and you've got a bargain there my friend'

It was with a growing feeling of unease that I handed over two ten pound notes and for some vague reason I was already regretting my purchase.

The 'thing' for want of a better name for it had an original price tag of £65 on it.

'Pick it up and take it, it's yours ' the man said, quickly pocketing my money and handing me a large used supermarket bag.

It was almost as if he was frightened to touch it.

And the look in his eyes told me he probably was.

*

It lay in the bag on the back seat of my car.

My eyes kept going to the review mirror fixed onto my windscreen.

The periodic jerking of the bag and its contents was because of the car's forward motion.

Of course it was.

Why the hell did I buy the strange thing in the first place? Maybe I should take it straight to the dump and..

Then why didn't I, why couldn't I, take it to the dump and put it where it...?

*

The bag and its contents were warm when I lifted it out of the car.

Of course it was, the interior of the car was warm, I had the heater full on..that would also explain the smell, the dank, musty smell.

What would Jenny say ?

*

'Wow' she said as she gently lifted the thing out of the crumpled shopping bag, her voice echoing in our newly, undecorated, yet to be furnished lounge.

'Our first bit of decoration'

I looked at her in utter amazement as she held the..*thing*.. at arms length, staring at its deformed face, its protruding teeth and grossly extended stomach.

'You like it?' My question hovered in the air unanswered as Jenny studied the obvious incredulous look that had settled on my face.

'She's beautiful' Jenny finally answered as she drew the ..*thing*.. closer and planted a tender kiss on its hairless forehead.

'She's beautiful' she repeated

Before I could bring myself to say a word, Jenny smiled, not at me but the at..*thing*..still in her grasp.

Her name is 'Yoola' Jenny said, walking across the bare wooden floorboards that led to the bare wooden stairs that led to our new bed and our new bedroom.

For reasons I could not explain, all of a sudden I did not want to be alone.

All alone.

'Jenny' I shouted after her...'Jenny, Yoola, please wait for me'.

Jonathan

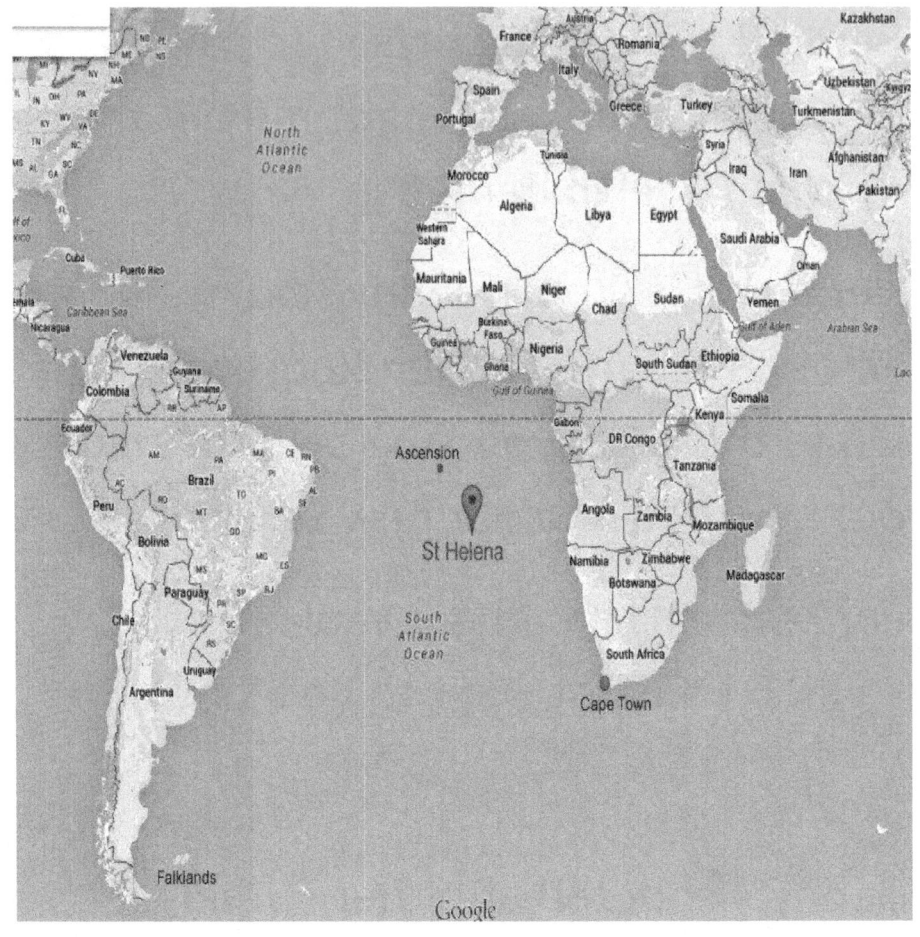

The six hour flight from Johannesburg to the tiny remote island which dared to pop its head up from the depths in the middle of the mighty South Atlantic Ocean was in some ways truly exciting and in other ways almost overwhelmingly terrifying.

We'd heard stories about the airport we were to land on at our destination, a mere strip of narrow concrete they called a runway squeezed between mountainous volcanic rocks and abruptly curtailed either end by steep cliffs falling steeply into the vast ocean itself.

St. Helena. Don't be surprised if you have never heard of it nor had the numerous Travel Agents we consulted.

If you were lucky enough to have been born on St. Helena you were affectionately known as a Saint.

As were my dear mother and grandparents and although all had been dead for a number years one of the main reasons for our two visits five years apart.

We had landed and my eyes were full of tears as the warm breeze of the Island wrapped itself around me and an overwhelming feeling of being 'home' filled my senses and invaded my soul. In the huge window of the airport building were a large crowd of people huddled together all vying for a place to be able to see for themselves their newly arrived visitors.

I looked back at the sea of welcoming faces and broad smiles, the faces of what I was about to discover, the faces of true Saints.

Through the airport building, the uniformed officials and gathered groups of soon to be realised distant relatives welcomed us to the Island with wide smiles and curious eyes..

Are they Saints or visitors? It matters not, they are with us now.

*

'There look, do you see it?'

Through the car's window and in the glare of the late afternoon sun we saw our first wire bird hopping between the low dunes of reddish sand and clustered shrubs. The panorama once off, probably the only asphalted road on the

Island, was one of the surrounding dead volcanic mountains, large areas of dusted grassland dotted with trees, wild hedgerows and snaking narrow unadopted lanes.

We had formerly arrived on the Island.

And our hugely unforgettable and ethereal meeting with Jonathan was imminent.

Plantation House

With eyes that have seen all this world has had to offer for over 190 years the proud and majestic giant tortoise watched my steady but slow approach, raising his long gnarled neck and standing tall in what I hoped was a friendly greeting.

When he slowly turned his head towards me I caught sight of the milky white of an age old cataract in his right eye. But more than this, much more, I sensed the incredible aura that completely enveloped this incredible creature.

'I am Jonathon' it seemed to say.

'You have come to visit we me, not I you'

It was then that I found myself on my hands and knees in the grass and Jonathon to my utter amazement and deep felt joy was moving step by step towards me, our heads level our noses getting closer and closer.

'You will move out of the way before I do'

His eyes spoke to me in no uncertain terms.

If a tortoise could smile Jonathon was smiling.

'You will move out of the before I do'

Jonathan, eyes repeated.

And then it was my privilege to move back, to obey the words of a being that was far older and indeed probably far wiser than I could ever hope to be.

We could not leave Plantation House or St.Helena Island before embracing the magnificent tortoise that was Jonathon and he was more than willing to allow us to do so.

Printed in Dunstable, United Kingdom